Out to Lunch

Peggy Perry Anderson

Green Light Readers

HOUGHTON MIFFLIN HARCOURT

BOSTON   NEW YORK

To Jack, Jorie, Jeffery and Jinger,
our nieces and nephews
who prepared us for parenthood.

Copyright © 1998 by Peggy Perry Anderson

First Green Light Readers edition 2015

All rights reserved. Originally published in hardcover in the United States by Houghton Mifflin
Books for Children, an imprint of Houghton Mifflin Harcourt Publishing Company, 1998.

For information about permission to reproduce selections from this book,
write to Permissions, Houghton Mifflin Harcourt Publishing Company,
215 Park Avenue South, New York, New York 10003.

Green Light Readers® and its logo are trademarks of HMH Publishers LLC,
registered in the United States and other countries.

www.hmhco.com

The Library of Congress cataloged the hardcover edition as follows:
Out to lunch/by Peggy Anderson
p. cm.
Summary: A mischievous frog makes a scene when his parents take him out
to a fancy restaurant to eat.
[Restaurants—Fiction. 2. Behavior—Fiction. 3. Frogs—Fiction. 4. Stories in rhyme.]
Title.
PZ8.3.A54840u

ISBN: 978-0-544-52858-1 paperback
ISBN: 978-0-544-56819-8 paper over board

Manufactured in China
SCP 10 9 8 7 6 5 4 3 2 1

4500535519

"Out to eat.
What a treat!"

"Too bad," Joe's mother said,
"our babysitter was sick in bed."

"We're ready to eat.
Just give us a seat!"

"Do you have crayons or playgrounds?"
asked Joe.

The waiter said no.

"Mind your manners well today.
We're out to lunch, not out to play."

"I'll have pie and cake.
NO PEAS!"

Mother said,
"One child's meal, please."

"I'm a reindeer!" said Joe.

"Now where did he go?"

"Peek-a-boo! I see you."

"Remember what I said today.
We're out to lunch, not out to play."

"Yippee! Yippee! Food for me!"

Joe slurped.

Joe burped.

"Uh-oh," said Joe.

"There's an itch on my toe."

"The table is no place for feet.
Please, Joe, sit still and eat."

Joe dropped his fork.

Joe dropped his spoon.

Joe launched his fish stick to the moon.

"JOE, SIT STILL!"

"Oh, dear. There's a fly in here!"

"Don't worry. I'll get him, Dad!"

WHAP!

ZAP!

"Best fly I ever had!"

"Okay, Joe, it's time to go."

"Out to eat. What a treat!"

12/15/15